ASHES OF THE MEMORIES

BlueRose ONE .com DIY
Stories Matter
NewDelhi • London

BLUEROSE PUBLISHERS
India | U.K.

BlueRose ONE
Stories Matter
New Delhi • London

For permissions requests or inquiries regarding this publication,
please contact:

BLUEROSE PUBLISHERS
www.BlueRoseONE.com
info@bluerosepublishers.com
+91 8882 898 898
+4407342408967

ISBN: 978-93-7542-877-0

First Edition: January 2026

PROLOGUE

Some stories are not meant to be told. They are written to be carried out.

I once believed that memory gradually fades away with time and silence could undo what heart has held tightly. Memories does not disappear but they seeps into your soul. It settles into the smallest corners of our lives, returning when we least expect it, unchanged and uninvited.

This story begins much after everything has already happened.

The moments that mattered most were not loud. They did not announce themselves as beginnings or endings. They arrived quietly—in glances held a second too long, in words almost spoken, in the comfort of knowing someone without ever fully having them.

Love, I have learned, is not always about staying. Sometimes it is about remaining—within pages, within thoughts, within the spaces we never fill again.

I did not write this to preserve happiness. I wrote it to understand loss.

These pages hold fragments: of conversations unfinished, of promises unmade, of emotions that refused to fade even when everything else did. If you read slowly, it is not because the story moves gently—it is because memory does.

This is not a tale of how love began. It is a record of what remained after it changed. And perhaps that is where all true stories start.

TABLE OF CONTENTS

- Ashes Of The Memories
- Words That Were Hers
- The Decision
- By The Lake
- The Photograph
- Beautifully Incomplete
- The Confession
- Just One Last Time
- Before The Last Petal Falls
- The Quiet Fear
- The Diagnosis
- The Beginning Of The End
- When Someone Finally Stays
- Closer Than I Realised
- A Goodbye Written In Ink
- The Last Look Of Love

EPIGRAPH

- **When a flower loses its petals, it loses its beauty- just like I will, once I lose you.**

- **Some love stories end unfinished,**

  Not because love was lacking,

  But because timing was.

ASHES OF THE MEMORIES

They say first love never leaves you. I laughed at that once. But when I saw my own words staring back at me from the pages of my debut novel, I realized — I had never left her. The world saw it as a love story. Only I knew it was my confession to Isha.

It had been ten years since we last spoke. Ten years since the arguments, the silence, and the inevitable goodbye. I built walls, and she built a life. That was supposed to be the end.

But memory is a strange thing. You think it disappears, but it seeps into your soul. You think it's gone, and then a song, a place, a sentence brings it rushing back. That's how she returned to me — not in person, but in the margins of my own book.

Every reader asked me, “Who is she?” I smiled and said, “Just a character.” But deep inside, I knew the truth: I had only ever written for one reader.

Her.

After hours of thought, I finally let the room slip into the arms of darkness. Silence enveloped me, and I found myself staring at her smile in the photographs scattered across my desk. Those memories, warm as a summer night, made my heart heavy and numb.

I lit a cigarette, and its flame illuminated her face in the photos as if time had flickered back to me. With every puff, I sank deeper into the beautiful ache of our memories — the walks by the lake on Thandi Sadak, the endless conversations, and the arguments that should have ended differently.

The cigarette collapsed into ashes. Just then, a notification popped up on my screen, breaking the silence: a reminder that I had to be at the literary fest in Haldwani by 11:00 a.m. tomorrow. For a moment, I stared at it as if it belonged to someone else’s life. Crowds,Questions, Applause. All of it seemed so distant from the quiet grief filling my room tonight.

I decided to leave Nainital by 9:00 a.m. The journey down the winding roads usually took an hour and a half, though in truth, it wasn’t the distance that worried me — it was the weight of the memories I would still be carrying.

When I finally sank into bed, exhaustion pulled at my body, but sleep refused to come. In one hand lay the stub of a broken cigarette, its smoke clinging to the room, and in my chest lay something far heavier: the remnants of her, alive not in reality, but in the grief I had never been able to bury.

Words that were hers

The next morning, I woke up and got ready for the literary fest. It was the first time my book, It Wasn't Meant For, had become a bestseller. Even with the success, my heart felt heavy with memories of Isha.

I never liked wearing formals or blazers, so I chose my usual blue denim jacket and headed out. Comfort always felt better than looking perfect.

The memories of Isha stayed with me like morning fog, soft but heavy. I decided I would text her — just one last time — after the fest.

As the car drove down the winding roads, I couldn't stop thinking about her. I wondered if she was still as beautiful as the meadows in bloom, wild and full of life, just like I remembered.

It rarely happened that I could talk for hours about something, but that day was different. After the long drive to Haldwani, I reached the fest and was welcomed with a huge round of applause. Then came the question — "How would you describe her, if she were real?"

I took a deep breath and answered with a few lines of poetry:

"Her remeberance cherish in my heart,

I wondered her glance as beautiful as meadows of flowers,

Glittering eyes deep black filled with joy and love,

Her loose waved hair were damn beautiful with the curls,

Delightful was she as a beautiful landscape could be,

Still cherishing in my heart as the barefoot walk on lush greenery..."

When I finished, the hall burst into another round of applause that lasted for minutes. Even now, I can still hear it in my mind. What they didn't know was that I hadn't described an imaginary character. I had described Isha. And in doing so, I had given away a piece of my heart.

As I stepped down from the stage, I was still thinking that maybe, in another world, Isha would have heard those words. But to my amazement, just a few moments later, I caught sight of a familiar face — half covered with a scarf — someone I had thought I would never see again.

That person slipped a folded note into my hand, and the moment I looked up, I froze. It was her. It was Isha.

In that instant, everything around me blurred. The applause, the chatter, the music — all of it faded until there was only her.

My heart filled with questions that crashed against each other: Why was she here? Had she really come for me? Or was it just fate playing a cruel trick?

After the literary fest, I should have returned home. But the exhaustion of the day weighed heavily on me, and perhaps — though I wouldn't admit it out loud — the faint 1% chance of meeting her again kept me from leaving. So instead of driving back, I checked into a small hotel nearby, letting the night of Haldwani hold me a little longer.

After checking into the hotel, I noticed the room's walls had been freshly whitewashed. A lone lamp glowed weakly beside the bed, and a small desk stood against the corner, almost inviting me to scatter Isha's photos across it and start a conversation with the ghosts of my past.

The incident at the fest — seeing her, even for a fleeting moment — clung to my heart like a shadow. I kept wondering how life might have been if we had stayed together. And then suddenly, I remembered the note. The note she had pressed into my hand today.

I reached into my pocket and pulled it out. My fingers hesitated before unfolding it. The moment I saw the handwriting, my chest tightened. Those slanting, curved letters — I knew them. They belonged to her. They belonged to Isha.

I read the words slowly, as if "*Some words don't belong to the world. They belong only to the two people who lived them. If you want to know more... meet me tomorrow at Naini Lake by 5 p.m.*"they might vanish before I reached the end:

I read those lines again and again, each time my pulse quickening. Was this real? Could fate truly be offering me another chance — or was it just a cruel trick, meant to reopen the wounds I had spent years trying to close?

THE DECISION

After a restless night at the hotel, I finally decided: I would meet Isha at the lake today, at 5:00 p.m. sharp.

I woke up at 6:00 a.m., restless, unable to wait. Within half an hour, I was already on my way to Nainital. I didn't want to take any risks — if this truly was my last chance to see her, I couldn't afford to miss it.

And yet, I couldn't ignore the irony. Destiny, or perhaps just my own flaws, had cursed me with a habit of being late to the moments that mattered most. That habit had cost me more than I ever expected. I still remember rushing to the hospital to see a friend, only to arrive too late — he was gone before I could say goodbye.

The weight of that memory pressed on me, so heavy that for a moment I almost forgot about Isha. My thoughts were interrupted by a knock at the door.

It was him — my only true companion since the day Isha and I had broken apart. He rushed inside, a little out of breath.

“Why did you call me so urgently?” he asked.

I hesitated, then told him everything — about the fest, about seeing Isha, and about the note that asked me to meet her at Naini Lake.

He stood silent for a long while, his eyes fixed on me. Finally, he said, “Don’t go.”

“Why?” I asked, my heart pounding.

“Because she’s your past,” he replied firmly. “And after so long, you can’t let the past ruin the present. She’s a memory — a painful one. Meeting her will only open old wounds.”

His words struck me, sharp and heavy. But my heart, already racing toward the lake, wasn’t ready to listen.

“Do you even realize what you’re saying?” I finally asked him. “For years I’ve carried her in my heart like a wound that refused to heal. And now, when fate places her back in front of me, you’re telling me to turn away?”

He sighed, rubbing his temples. "I'm saying this because I know what you went through. I watched you break once, and I don't want to see you shatter again."

Then he left the room, but his words — She's your past… she'll only open old wounds — kept circling in my mind. My heart was still restless, caught in confusion.

I sat down, the note trembling in my hand. Closing my eyes, I let the silence push me toward a decision. One thought rose above the noise inside me: If I walk away now, I'll spend the rest of my life wondering what might have been.

When I opened my eyes again, the clock showed past 10:00 a.m. The day was moving forward, and so was my choice.

I pressed the note to my chest, breathing deeply. I knew the risk. I knew the pain waiting at the other end. But regret was the heaviest burden I had ever carried — and I wasn't willing to add another stone to that weight.

"I'll go," I whispered to myself.

BY THE LAKE

And finally, the moment arrived — the time to meet her. I got ready, but one thought kept circling my mind: should I take flowers for her? In the end, I chose to go empty-handed, believing it would be best to keep things simple, honest.

I reached the lake, and, as always, I was late. Yet to my amazement, she was there.

My lips trembled, and I whispered her name, "Isha."

At first, she didn't notice me. But as I walked closer, she suddenly turned, and before I could gather my thoughts, she hugged me. For almost a minute, she held me tightly, as if she had been waiting for this moment even more eagerly than I had.

I stood there, nervous and quiet, unable to understand what was happening, my heart pounding louder than the ripples of the lake beside us.

When she finally pulled back, I caught a glimpse of her eyes. They were the same — deep, dark, carrying a world within them. But there was something else too… a hint of weariness, as though time had quietly left its shadows there.

Neither of us spoke at first. The silence between us was heavy, yet alive — filled with all the unsaid words from the years we had lost. Finally, I managed to say, "You… you really came."

She smiled faintly and replied, "And you… you're still late?"

That small tease, so ordinary, carried the weight of a thousand memories. For a brief second, it felt as though nothing had changed — as though we were still the same two people who once laughed together under open skies.

But then, reality crept back in. Questions crowded my heart, and I could see in her eyes that she carried her own.

"Isha," I said softly, "why now? After all this time?"

She turned toward the shimmering water, her gaze distant. "Because some stories don't end… no matter how much we try to bury them. And ours… ours was one of them."For the first time in my life, despite being an author, I had no words left to speak.

The photograph

The day drifted on, and time seemed to slip through our hands. Gradually, the sky turned pink, as though it too was blushing at the sight of us together again after ten long years.

We sat side by side by the lake, neither of us uttering a word. The silence wasn't empty — it was heavy, filled with all the emotions I had carried within me for years, yet couldn't bring myself to voice. I wanted to ask her a hundred questions, but none left my lips.

Instead, she quietly reached into her bag and handed me something — a photograph.

It was of us, standing side by side at the old Wilderness Church of Nainital. My arm rested easily around her shoulder, and her smile lit up the frame. We looked happy, effortlessly so, as if the moment had belonged to a fairy tale that would never end.

My breath caught. Of all the things I had imagined that day, this was not one of them. I never thought I would receive a gift on our first meeting after so long — and certainly not this. It felt like she had handed me back a piece of my own heart.

By then, the sky had darkened, the lake shimmering in the fading light. Gathering my courage, I finally asked, "Shall we go to our old snacking place?"

She shook her head gently. "Not today," she said, her voice soft. "But tomorrow… same time, same place. We'll talk then. I should be going now."

I wanted to hold onto the moment, to stop her from leaving again. But instead, I simply nodded, watching her walk away — leaving me with a photograph, a promise, and a silence that felt louder than words.

With the photograph clutched tightly in my hand, I walked back home carrying a strange mix of joy, confusion, and nostalgia. Every step I took seemed lighter, yet my heart weighed heavily with questions.

All evening, my thoughts circled only around her. Perhaps it had always been my favorite pastime — thinking about Isha. And tonight, after so many years, it didn't feel like a habit of longing but a quiet reunion within my own soul.

The night unfolded like one of the best I had ever lived. Her face lingered in my mind, the photograph rested beside me like a piece of the past made real again, and her promise — tomorrow, same time, same place — glowed brighter than any star outside my window.

Yet, as I lay in bed, staring into the dark, doubt crept in. Would she truly come back tomorrow? Or was this all just a fleeting moment, a gift meant to be cherished only once? I didn't know what the next day would bring, but I knew it would change everything.

Beautifully incomplete

The next morning, I woke to a strange sweetness in the air — a freshness that felt almost like love itself. The flowers bloomed brighter in the autumn sun, the birds sang more melodiously, and the dawn sky glowed red, as if reflecting the fire in my heart.

And all of this — all this beauty — felt like it existed because of a single photograph and a promise. Yet beneath the joy, one question still gnawed at me: Would she come?

By evening, I found myself at the lake once again. For once, I arrived early — a few minutes before five. And to my amazement, she was already there, waiting.

In that moment, something shifted inside me. Perhaps she, too, had begun to rediscover the feelings we once thought were lost.

The first thing she did was embrace me — a tight, unhesitating hug. And then, with a smile, she asked me to go with her to our favorite café, to sit for hours like before.

But her hug… it was different. For a second, it felt as though she had pulled me out of myself. I froze, caught between past and present, unable to respond.

Still, holding myself together, I agreed. As we walked toward the café, the same scenes from a decade ago seemed to replay. I even thought of plucking a flower for her, as I used to — but something deep inside stopped me.

We chose the same corner table by the window, overlooking the bustling street. She sat across from me, her face half in the glow of the evening light. I just stared, not at her beauty, but at the strange comfort of her presence.

"So…" she said at last, her fingers lightly tracing the rim of her cup, "you still order the same?"

I smiled faintly. "Old habits die hard… but I've left coffee."

Her brows rose in surprise. "You? Leaving coffee? Why?"

I leaned back, glancing out of the window before answering softly, "Because some things are meant to be left at a beautiful point. Some things… are beautifully incomplete."

She studied me for a long moment, then repeated quietly, "Beautifully incomplete… You still talk in riddles."

I gave a hollow chuckle. "Maybe because words have been my only way of surviving without you."

Silence pressed between us, filled by the hum of strangers and faint music drifting through the café.

Finally, she whispered, "Do you know how many times I wanted to come back?"

My heart skipped. I leaned forward. "Then why didn't you?"

Her eyes glistened as she looked up. "Because sometimes love isn't enough. Back then… everything was falling apart. We were young, stubborn. And I was afraid — afraid that if I stayed, we'd destroy each other."

Her words hit me like a storm. I swallowed hard, my voice breaking. "And do you think walking away didn't destroy me?"

Her lips trembled, but she didn't look away. "It destroyed me too. Every single day."

For a moment, I couldn't speak. The pain I thought was mine alone — she had carried it too, quietly, all these years.

"Ten years, Isha," I said in a low voice. "Ten years I've lived with questions and not one answer. Do you know what it feels like to bleed and never stop?"

Her fingers reached across the table, hesitating before resting near mine. "Do you think I don't?"

The evening light shifted, painting her face in shades of gold and shadow. And for the first time, I realized — we were not just two people meeting again. We were two broken halves, carrying the same wound, still wondering if it could ever heal.

And as we walked back from the café, the silence between us wasn't heavy anymore — it was gentle, almost like an old friend walking beside us. Before we parted, she turned to me, her voice softer than I had ever heard it.

"Promise me," she said, "that you'll meet me here every day."

I nodded without hesitation. "I promise."

Her eyes lingered on mine for a moment before she slipped something into my hand — a folded letter.

"Read it only when you reach home," she whispered.

I agreed, though my curiosity burned with every step. After dropping her off, I walked back to my home, the letter pressed tightly in my palm.

That night, as I sat alone, I held it under the dim light — the weight of her words yet unopened, but already changing everything inside me.

THE CONFESSION

I unfolded the letter in my hands, my fingers trembling slightly as I did. The words on the page were carefully written—the kind I had always treasured and loved reading. But now, they felt like a cruel surprise. Each sentence struck me harder than I expected, and a deep ache spread through my chest. My heart felt as if it had shattered into pieces that could never be put back together.

The letter re'ealed Isha's marriage, which was only three months away. The reality of it hit me suddenly, like the ground had slipped from beneath my feet. My chest ached, my lips trembled, and I felt a wave of helpless sadness I could not control. Memories of her—our moments together, her laughter, the warmth of her presence—came rushing back, making the pain even sharper.

In that instant, I was pulled back into the same lonely, empty state I had known before I met her. The joy and hope I once held seemed gone, replaced by a hollow ache that reminded me how fragile happiness can be. I was left alone with my heartbreak, knowing that the future I had imagined with her would never come to be.

Sitting at my table, I poured myself a glass of wine, lit a cigarette, and thought of Isha with every successive puff. One question refused to leave my mind: if she was getting married in three months, why did she still want to meet me every day?

Restless, I called a friend and told him everything. He reminded me that he had already warned me not to see Isha. When I asked what I should do next, he told me to move on, to forget her like a dream that was never meant for me. But my heart would not listen; it kept urging me to see her again.

The Inner conflict grew stronger, pulling me deeper into love for her. I ended the call, lit another cigarette, and went to bed. That night passed in restless silence. The next day, after wasting away the hours at home, I finally went out to meet her in the evening. This time, not to the lake, but to the path near Dorothy's seat. She hadn't arrived yet, so I waited. After a few minutes, I saw her—dressed in a beautiful green dress that made me forget all my worries, if only for a moment.

Today, she didn't hug me. Instead, she handed me a flower, just as I used to give her. For a moment, I was at a loss for words. We walked together in silence, and at last, I asked her about the note. She looked down and quietly admitted that she was marrying someone else.

I asked her what was going through her mind, and tears welled up in her eyes. Seeing her cry was the most painful thing I could ever imagine. I let her calm down, and after a while, she finally spoke. Though it felt like something out of a fairy tale, she confessed softly, “I love you. I realized it only after reading your books and seeing that you haven’t moved on yet.”

In that moment, time seemed to stop. My heart ached with both love and sorrow. There she stood, fragile yet radiant, and I knew I loved her more than ever—even though she was a dream I could never truly keep.

Just one last time

After everything — after hearing her confess that she still loved me — I made my decision. I would leave her. Not because I wanted to, but because I believed she deserved freedom from the burden of my love, from the weight of words that kept pulling her back to me.

I told myself I would never see her again. That was the only way to set her free.

But fate is cruel in its timing. My phone rang, and there it was — her message. “Meet me at the lake. Today. 5 p.m.”

For a long while, I sat frozen, my heart and mind locked in battle. Walk away, or go? End it, or give in?

Finally, I whispered to myself, almost like a prayer: "Just one last time."

The lake shimmered beneath the evening sun. I stood at the edge, my heart pounding, the words one last time echoing inside me — a warning, a plea, a prayer.

And then I saw her.

Isha stood there, waiting. For a moment, time folded. She looked just as she did the first day we met, though the shadows beneath her eyes told the story of the years between us.

When our eyes met, she smiled faintly. No words. No explanations. Just that smile — fragile, but real.

This time, she didn't hug me. The silence stretched until I finally said, "You came."

She nodded softly. "Some goodbyes can't be written in letters. Or said on calls."

Her words stole the little happiness I had carried over the past few days. It slipped through me in an instant.

After a long pause, I asked, "Why tell me you loved me… only to leave me again?"

Her gaze drifted to the horizon. "Because it was the truth. And I couldn't let you live without knowing it. But love… love doesn't change what's coming."

Her honesty cut deeper than any lie could. I wanted to hold her, to beg her to stay, but my body refused to move.

"Isha," I whispered, my voice breaking, "one last time… say it again."

Her eyes glistened as they met mine. And with trembling lips, she spoke the words that healed and destroyed me all at once:

"I love you."

The world fell silent. The lake, the wind, the sky — everything seemed to hold still, as if bearing witness to the end of a story that refused to end.

Before the last petal falls

From the very next day, even after telling myself again and again not to meet her, I finally gave in to my heart.

Maybe, I thought, I should see her — not to make our goodbye harder, but to make it easier for her to move on, slowly and peacefully, from me.

That evening, I decided that when I met her, I would ask her to relive all the memories we once shared — not as lovers, but as two people saying goodbye to what they once had.

When I reached the lake, she was sitting alone on the old bench, lost in her thoughts. In her hand, she held a flower and was gently plucking its petals one by one.

Curious, I asked softly, “What are you doing, Isha?”

She looked up and gave me a faint smile.

“I’ve decided to pluck one flower every day until everything between us ends,” she said. “When a flower loses its petals, it loses its beauty — just like I will, once I lose you. But the hardest part,” she paused, her voice shaking, “is always the last petal. Because that’s when it really ends.”

For a moment, I couldn’t speak. Her words hit me hard — they were painful, but still beautiful.

I wanted to stop her, to hold her hand and tell her that love never truly fades — but the look in her eyes told me she already understood that.

Her words stayed with me. And in that moment, I made a decision — I would make the remaining days before her marriage the happiest days of her life.

Without saying a word, I took her hand and led her uphill to one of my favourite places — a spot where I often sat alone, watching the sun set and the stars appear one by one.

As we climbed higher, the air turned cooler, and the world below began to fade away. When we finally reached the top, the sky was glowing orange, slowly turning dark, and stars started to twinkle above us.

She looked at me curiously. “Why have you brought me here?”

I smiled and said softly, “Because after you, this is my favourite place. I thought maybe… it could become yours too.”

We sat quietly for a while, looking at the sky. Then I finally spoke what I had kept inside for so long.

“Isha,” I said, “I don’t want to stay incomplete forever. All I want is you — by my side, no matter what happens.”

For a moment, she said nothing. Then she slowly stood up and whispered, “I should go… it’s getting late.”

Before I could say anything more, she walked away — leaving me there under the stars, holding a silence that said everything our words couldn’t.

THE QUIET FEAR

Later that night, when I returned home, I found a letter lying on my desk. Surprised, I asked my mother who had brought it. She said softly, “A girl came by. She told me to give this to you.”

For a moment, my heart skipped a beat. I knew before even opening it who it was from.

It was Isha.

Her familiar handwriting covered the envelope, neat and graceful, just as I remembered. With trembling hands, I unfolded the letter and began to read.

She had written:

"Sometimes, not all beautiful things stay incomplete. Some of them do find their way to completion – in their own quiet way."

I read those lines again and again, her words echoing in my mind until they blurred into my thoughts. My heart was in turmoil – I didn't know what to think, what to feel.

On one side, the idea of being with her forever bloomed inside me like spring flowers, soft and full of hope. But on the other, reality pressed hard against my chest – the thought of her marriage, of the distance that still stood between us, and the question that haunted me most:

How could I help her move on… when I was still lost in her myself?

The next morning felt strangely heavy. The sunlight slipped weakly through the curtains, yet everything around me seemed dim.

Maybe it was the sleepless night, or maybe it was the weight of her words still echoing in my head: "Sometimes, not all beautiful things stay incomplete."

I didn't know what she meant exactly – hope, promise, or goodbye. But her letter had stirred something inside me, something I wasn't ready to name.

I tried to focus on my writing, but my hands felt weak, and the words wouldn't come. The pen slipped from my fingers twice before I gave up and leaned back in my chair.

A dull pain spread across my chest – faint, but enough to leave me breathless for a few seconds.

I brushed it off. "Just tired," I told myself. Maybe too many sleepless nights, too many thoughts that refused to rest.

The next evening, I met Isha again by the lake. She smiled when she saw me, though her eyes looked tired too – maybe from thinking as much as I had.

"You look pale," she said, a hint of worry in her voice.

I smiled faintly. "I'm fine. Just… overworked, maybe."

She frowned, unconvinced, but didn't press further. Instead, she began talking about her day -her family, the plans for her wedding, small stories that carried the comfort of normal life.

I listened quietly, though each word felt distant, like hearing life through a thin wall of glass.

At one point, she reached for a small notebook in her bag and handed it to me. "You once said writing heals you," she said softly. "So, write again. Even if it hurts."

Her words felt like a whisper from fate. I smiled, took the notebook, and said, "Maybe I will. Maybe it's time to finish what I started."

Over the next few days, the pain became more frequent – first a tired ache, then something sharper, deeper.

But I didn't tell her. I didn't want to add my suffering to her worries. She already carried too much in her heart.

Instead, I met her as always — the same smile, the same quiet walks, pretending everything was fine.

But sometimes, when she laughed, I'd find myself staring – trying to memorize every curve of her smile, every sound of her voice, as if storing them for a time when I might not have them anymore.

And somewhere deep down, a quiet fear began to grow – a fear I refused to name.

The diagnosis

The next few days slipped by in silence. The pain that once came and went now stayed longer, sharp enough to make me pause mid-sentence or lose my breath for a moment. I had become good at hiding it – or at least, I thought I had.

Each evening, I still met Isha by the lake. She would talk, smile, sometimes even tease me for being so quiet. But she didn't know that half the time, my silence was not out of thought – it was to steady my breathing.

One evening, when she handed me a cup of tea, my hand trembled slightly. She noticed.

"Are you sure you're okay?" she asked, concern clouding her eyes.

I smiled weakly. "I'm fine, Isha. Just the cold breeze."

But I knew it wasn't the breeze. The ache in my chest felt deeper, heavier – as if it was not in my heart, but behind it.

The next morning, my mother found me sitting at my desk, half-asleep over my notes. I had been coughing all night, though I tried to hide it.

She looked at me with that quiet worry only a mother has. "You're going to the doctor today," she said.

I wanted to argue, to tell her it was nothing – but even speaking felt heavier than usual.

So, I nodded. "Alright."

At the hospital, time seemed to slow. The doctor's calm voice broke through my thoughts. "We'll need to run a few tests," he said gently. "It might be nothing serious, but we should be sure."

I waited for hours – long enough for every possibility to run through my head. When he finally returned with the results, his face said everything before his words did.

He sat down across from me and spoke quietly, almost carefully, as if choosing every word.

"It's stage three," he said. "We'll begin treatment as soon as possible."

For a moment, everything blurred – his voice, the sound of people in the hallway, even the ticking clock on the wall. It all faded into silence.

Stage three.

Three simple words – and the world as I knew it changed.

On the way back home, I kept thinking about Isha. Her smile. Her letters. The way she plucked petals as if counting down days she didn't even know were numbered.

A strange calm filled me – not fear, not anger, just a quiet realization.

Maybe, I thought, this is how life completes the stories we never could.

That evening, I didn't go to the lake. I just sat by the window, watching the world darken outside. My unfinished manuscript lay open on the desk -the one I had promised myself I'd finish someday.

And for the first time, I whispered to it,

"Looks like we're running out of somedays."

THE BEGINNING OF THE END

I had finally decided to finish my manuscript. But deep inside, I also made another decision — I would never see Isha again. Everything that once felt like a beginning was slipping away again, like fog dissolving in morning light. Hope was fading, and all I had left was my book — a final gift, something she could hold even when I would no longer be able to stay.

Maybe that was the only part of me allowed to love her anymore.

As I sat at my desk, trying to write, a notification suddenly lit up my screen. My heart skipped — but it wasn't her.

It was Siya. Siya and I had not known each other for very long, yet the bond we shared felt different—deep in a quiet, unspoken way. We could feel each other's pain. For the first time, I found solace in someone other than Isha, not because there was love between us, but because there was affection of a rare kind. The kind that exists only with a few people—those who do not enter your life to be loved, but to offer the support and comfort the heart waits for throughout its journey.

She asked for the photographs I had taken of her for my previous book cover. I sent them instantly and she thanked me, trying to start a small conversation — but my replies were mechanical, hollow. My thoughts could not left Isha.

Even the silence in the room echoed her absence.

Every word I tried to write became her name. Every page began with a memory I was trying to forget. And yet, the more I tried to push her out of my mind, the more she ruled it — like she always had, even years after goodbye.

A strange loneliness settled in. The kind that doesn't hurt loudly… but quietly, in every breath.

And so I wrote — not to finish a book, but to stop myself from falling apart before she walked into a new life where I no longer existed.

And as far as I knew, this was meant to be a new beginning for me — a chance to finally rise above my past. Or perhaps, it was a new ending in disguise… one that quietly hinted at another start I was too afraid to imagine.

The pressure of my thoughts grew unbearable. I pushed my manuscript aside, letting the pages rest where my heart couldn't. I stepped out for a cigarette, hoping the smoke would calm the storm inside me — or at least give me a moment to breathe without the weight of her name pressing on my chest.

Under the faint glow of the streetlight, the silence wrapped around me. I inhaled deeply, as if each breath was a desperate attempt to steady myself against all the chaos I could no longer control.

All I needed… was a pause from the war happening inside my head.

But the pause didn't last long.

The moment the cigarette burned out, reality returned — heavier than before. I stared at the dying ember between my fingers and couldn't help thinking how easily things fade… how quickly warmth turns into smoke.

I flicked the ash away and leaned against the cold wall behind me, letting my head rest back. Above me, the night sky stretched endlessly — dark, silent, uncaring. And yet, I found myself searching it for answers I knew I would never find.

My phone buzzed again.

Not a message — just a reminder:

"Finish the final chapter."

The irony almost made me smile.

If only hearts came with reminders like that —

"Finish healing."

"Don't look back."

"Forget her."

But hearts don't listen. Not to reason. Not to reminders.

With a reluctant sigh, I returned to my desk. The pages waited for me — untouched, expectant — like chapters of a life that no longer belonged to me.

I picked up the pen, but my hand trembled slightly. I wasn't sure if it was the cold… or the fear that the ending I wrote for my characters would never match the ending I wanted for us.

My eyes drifted to the only photograph on my wall — the one I had never taken down. The curve of her smile still felt like home, even from a distance of years.

A whisper escaped my lips, softer than the turning of a page:

"Isha… how do I let you go?"

There was no answer — only the quiet rustle of papers and the lingering scent of smoke.

I closed my eyes and let the silence speak for me.

Maybe tomorrow would be different.

Maybe I'd wake up with less of her and more of me.

Or maybe…

Maybe tomorrow would pull me closer to the fate I had been running from all along.

When someone finally stays

Lost in silence, my thoughts drifted toward a future I couldn't imagine. That's when my phone rang – Siya.

We had never been close enough to call it a bond, yet I answered.

And somehow, that night stretched into hours.

We talked… really talked –

About our lives,

Our failures, our fears, the kind of conversation only two lonely hearts can have

When something fragile and unnamed begins to grow between them.

Her laughter filled the spaces where loneliness had been living for so long.

Her voice kept me anchored to a world I was slowly slipping away from.

By the time the clock struck 4 a.m., my walls had begun to crumble. Emotion overpowered caution.

And before I could stop myself, I told her the truth –

About the diagnosis, About the countdown

I had been hiding from everyone, including myself.

The line went quiet. But for the first time in a long while…

I didn't feel alone in that silence.

I could hear her breathing – steady, soft –

As if choosing every breath with care, searching for words where none existed.

Then finally, in a voice warmer than dawn, she asked:

"Why didn't you tell anyone?"

How could I explain that silence sometimes hurts less than expectations?

That when hope keeps slipping, your voice slips with it too?

"I didn't want to be someone's burden," I whispered.

Something broke in her tone when she replied, "Don't ever think that again."

Her words hit a part of me I thought had died long ago. She wasn't crying –

But the ache beneath her calm felt like a tear my heart noticed.

"Listen," she said, almost fiercely, "You're not alone in this. Not anymore."

I swallowed the sudden warmth that rushed into my chest. How could someone I barely knew suddenly care so much? How could her concern feel stronger than the love I had carried for years?

A strange guilt crept in – As if letting her in meant betraying the memory of Isha…

Or whatever was left of it.

But Siya didn't ask for a place in my heart. She simply found the broken spaces and stood there quietly, refusing to leave.

We talked again – softer this time – About fear, about fate, about how life sometimes ruins the stories we dream of writing.

And somewhere between her pauses and my breathing, a tiny shift happened –

Small, but undeniable.

Before hanging up, she whispered,

"If the night ever feels too heavy… call me. I'll stay awake for you."

Long after the call ended, I stared at the screen, wondering how someone had found me in the ruins I didn't know were visible.

For the first time in forever, The night didn't feel endless. There was fear.

There was pain. But there was also…Someone. Someone who didn't run.

Someone who stayed.

Closer than I realised

Days slipped by, and slowly my manuscript transformed into something I never intended. Between the chapters of Isha and the shadows of my memories, another name began to appear — Siya. Not as a distraction anymore… but as a presence I was learning to depend on.

Our bond deepened without warning.

Late-night talks turned into shared mornings.

Concern turned into comfort.

And comfort… into something that felt dangerously close to love.

For the first time in years, someone wasn't a memory — she was real.

She was here.

But love — or anything like it — carries its own fears.

I noticed the shift before I understood it.

Her calls became shorter.

Her replies delayed.

Her voice — once filled with light — carried hesitation now.

The girl who once promised to stay awake for me was suddenly too busy to pick up the phone.

It was subtle — but pain doesn't need to be loud to be felt.

A heaviness settled in my chest, not just from the illness growing inside me, but from the distance growing in her eyes.

As if destiny was reminding me: Don't forget… some hearts are not meant for you.

Doctor visits continued, therapies and medications blending into meaningless routines but the real ache wasn't in my diagnosis — It was in the fear that I was losing hope again.

One evening, I confronted the silence between us.

“Is everything okay?” I asked her over the phone, trying to hide the tremble in my voice.

She breathed out slowly — too slowly — as if holding back a truth that had been waiting to spill.

“There’s something I never told you,” she said.

My heart stalled in that moment. She continued, voice fragile:

“I didn’t step into your life by coincidence.

I knew about you… long before you told me.”

My fingers tightened around the phone.

“Isha told me everything,” she whispered,

“your books, your breakup… and even your illness.”

For a moment, time felt still — silent, mercilessly still.

Every beat of my heart turned into a question.

Siya paused, gathering courage.

“I was asked to stay away…but I couldn’t.”

Those words struck deeper than any confession of love.

She knew my story.

She knew my scars.

She knew the ending I was walking toward.

And still… she came closer.

But now she was afraid —not of my illness, but of losing control of her own heart.

“I didn’t mean to feel this much,” she admitted.

The call ended with a promise and a fear:

“I’m here… but I don’t know for how long.”

After she hung up, the silence returned —but it wasn’t empty anymore.

It was filled with truth.

Pain, yes.

Fear, yes.

But also something else — A love that wasn’t supposed to happen…

Yet did.

A GOODBYE WRITTEN IN INK

It was just two days left for Isha's marriage when my phone rang again. This time, it was my doctor.

He asked casually about my book —how far I had reached, whether I would finish it in time.

I told him, with a tired smile he couldn't see,

"I just need to finish a few stanzas…I'll be done by tonight. I want to give it to Isha on her wedding day."

There was a pause on the other end, a silence that didn't feel medical anymore —it felt personal… heavy.

"Neil," he finally spoke, his voice softer than ever,

"As per your latest reports…I need you to know the truth."

I didn't breathe. I didn't move.

"You don't have much time left," he said gently.

"Maybe a few days…maybe only a few hours."

The words fell into me like stones into a deep lake—sinking fast, rippling everything.

But instead of breaking down, instead of crying or screaming at fate, I simply smiled — a helpless, quiet smile.

"Thank you, Doctor," was all I said before cutting the call.

Not because it didn't hurt…but because I had no space left inside me for one more heartbreak.

And now, more than anything,

I just wanted to finish those last lines — before my story ended without a final page.

The night felt endless as I wrote the last line of my manuscript — the book that carried her name in every silent breath between the words. My hands trembled, not from fear anymore, but from the urgency of time slipping away inside me.

This wasn't a love story anymore.

This was my goodbye.

As the first light of dawn brushed against the window, I closed the book gently — almost afraid it would break if I touched it too firmly. My heartbeat slowed for a moment, as if even my body understood… this was the last thing I needed to finish before I left.

I didn't go to Isha's house. I didn't dare.

Instead, I went to see Siya.

She opened the door, surprised — still wearing the confusion in her sleepy eyes. Before she could ask anything, I handed her the manuscript. The weight of the book seemed heavy in her hands… or maybe it was the weight of what it carried inside.

"Please," I said quietly, "give this to Isha on her wedding day."

She froze — hurt flickering in her eyes, a thousand unspoken questions rising and dying in her throat. I could see her struggling to understand, to hold onto me, to not let everything collapse like broken promises.

I didn't give her the chance to speak.

I placed my hand gently over hers — the one holding the book.

"And… both of you," I whispered, "read it that day."

Her lips parted, maybe to stop me, maybe to ask me why…but I stepped back before she could say a word.

For once, I didn't look back for permission, for hope, for a reason to stay.

I walked away.

My footsteps felt final — each one echoing the truth I was trying so hard not to show:

This wasn't just a gift.

It was the last piece of me she would ever hold.

Siya's voice called out from behind me, just once:

"Neil… why does this feel like goodbye?"

I paused for a heartbeat —just one.

Then I forced a smile she couldn't see, and kept walking.

Because if I turned back…every broken part of me would beg to stay alive a little longer.

I couldn't afford that. The day was rising, life was moving forward, and I was disappearing quietly with the darkness.

No dramatic confessions.

No final embraces.

No last-minute miracles.

Just a boy, his unfinished heart, and a book that now carried everything he could no longer say.

The last look of love

The day of Isha's wedding arrived like a cruel reminder that life doesn't pause — not even for dying promises. The city was busy celebrating a love story, while mine was quietly reaching its final page.

That morning, the pain inside my chest refused to stay silent. Darkness pulled at the edges of my vision as my body finally surrendered. My mother rushed me to the hospital, fear trembling in her hands. The beeping machines, the sterile white walls, the cold oxygen mask — everything blurred together, a fading picture I could hardly recognize.

The doctors whispered urgently, moving around me, trying to bargain with time but death does not listen to medicine and as consciousness flickered in and out, a single thought anchored me:

Did they read it yet?

Meanwhile, miles away, Isha glowed in her bridal red — beautiful enough to make time jealous. Just before the ceremony, Siya approached her, clutching the manuscript I had given her. Her hands trembled as she spoke, "He wanted you to have this… today."

Isha froze.

The sight of my handwriting hit her like a forgotten memory returning all at once. Side by side, beneath the wedding lights, they opened the book that held my heart.

The first dedication read:

To the girl who taught me love — Isha,

Thank you for every smile that made my world worth living.

I will always love you — in every life.

Her breath collapsed into tears. She turned the page and another dedication awaited—one that led Siya into silence:

And to the girl who stayed — Siya,

I never expected you. But you became the hope I thought I had lost.

If I ever get another chance at life… I hope I meet you first.

Siya's tears fell fast — heartbreak and love intertwined.

Then they reached the final lines:

By the time you hold this book,

I may only have a day or two left.

But don't cry for me — I am leaving with love in both hands.

Their hearts stopped together and the bouquet slipped from Isha's grip and shattered the silence of the hall. Without a single thought for guests, rituals, or destiny, they both ran — not toward a wedding aisle, but toward the boy who loved them enough to write them into eternity.

The hospital door flew open. They found me lying quietly, peacefully — as if I had been waiting just for them. My eyes fluttered open, barely able to hold the vision before me: the first love of my life on one side… and the last light of my heart on the other.

Isha held my face, tears falling faster than words.

"This isn't your ending… please," she begged.

Siya took my hand gently, voice trembling, "You promised to fight…"

With the last bit of strength left inside me, I smiled — a soft, grateful smile.

"Don't be sad," I whispered faintly, "…I'm not leaving empty anymore."

My chest rose one final time… A soft breath. A peaceful one.

Like a sentence that no longer needs a full stop.

And then —Silence. Not painful. Not lonely. Just peaceful.

A boy, his last smile, and two girls who finally knew how much they meant to him.

EPILOGUE

The lake was quiet again.

Weeks had passed since the wedding, since the hospital, since the words that had ended everything and yet refused to leave. Life had moved forward — as it always does — indifferent to love and loss alike.

Siya stood by the water, holding the book against her chest.

The cover was worn now, the pages touched too many times to remain new. People had begun to read it — strangers who would never know the weight behind each word. They called it a love story. Some called it tragic. Few understood that it was, above all, a goodbye.

She opened the book once more, not to read, but to feel.

Inside, between the lines, he was still there — in the pauses, in the unfinished sentences, in the quiet spaces where his voice had learned how to rest.

She reached into her bag and took out a flower Slowly and gently she let a single petal fall into the lake. It floated for a moment, then drifted away — not lost, only changed.

Some love stories do not stay. They remain. Siya closed the book. And for the first time, she did not feel alone.

AUTHOR'S NOTE

This novella is a work of fiction.

It was born not from events, but from emotions — the kind that linger long after moments pass. The characters, places, and conversations within these pages are imagined, yet the feelings they carry are deeply human.

Ashes of the Memories is not meant to offer answers, resolutions, or perfect endings. It is an exploration of what remains when love changes form — when it is no longer lived, but remembered.

Writing this story was an act of listening — to silence, to absence, and to the quiet resilience of the heart. If these pages felt slow at times, it is because some emotions do not rush. If they felt heavy, it is because memory carries weight.

To every reader who found a part of themselves here — in the longing, the loss, or the hope — thank you for reading with patience and openness.

Some stories are not meant to be closed.

They are meant to be carried.